D1284533

Praise for <u>The Power in</u>

"*The Power in Me* offers an invaluable reminder to us all: to be still, to breathe, and to recognize the strength within us. This gentle reminder about mindfulness will find a home at story times and bedtimes."

—Matthew C. Winner, school librarian
and host of *The Children's Book Podcast*

"We all have the power to manage our stress and anxious thoughts. This book will help children and adults remember to breathe through anxiety, knowing that every emotion eventually passes. An inspirational book to share with the children in our lives."

—Connie Bowman, actress, yoga teacher, and
author of *Back to Happy*, *Beau's Day Care Day*,
There's an Elephant in My Bathtub, and *Super Socks*

"Written in lovely rhyme with adorable illustrations, *The Power in Me* is a fantastic book, empowering children through relatable language that is a joy to read and easy to understand. Schools and libraries need more books like this!"

—Elena Reznikova, author of *Thank You, Me*

"Through rhyming verse and colorful artwork, Ms. Axel invites her readers to find feelings of peace, calm, and well-being through the secret power of breath. Simple, interactive steps empower children to not only understand the nature of their thoughts and emotions, but to experience the transformative effects of short, guided breathing exercises. *The Power in Me* is sure to appeal to educators and caregivers searching for an accessible and kid-friendly introduction to mindfulness."

—Paula Smith, school psychologist and certified
dynamic mindfulness/transformative life
skills trainer for Niroga Institute

Sophie ~
May you always
find your power!
♡ Meaghan Axel

The POWER in Me

Story by **MEAGHAN AXEL**

Illustrations by **MICHELLE SIMPSON**

BELLE ISLE BOOKS
www.belleislebooks.com

Copyright © 2020 by Meaghan Axel

No part of this book may be reproduced in any form or by any electronic or mechanical means, or the facilitation thereof, including information storage and retrieval systems, without permission in writing from the publisher, except in the case of brief quotations published in articles and reviews. Any educational institution wishing to photocopy part or all of the work for classroom use, or individual researchers who would like to obtain permission to reprint the work for educational purposes, should contact the publisher.

ISBN: 978-1-947860-83-4
LCCN: 2019912302

Designed by Michael Hardison

Project managed by Haley Simpkiss

Printed in the United States of America

Published by

Belle Isle Books (an imprint of Brandylane Publishers, Inc.)

5 S. 1st Street

Richmond, Virginia 23219

belleislebooks.com | brandylanepublishers.com

BELLE ISLE BOOKS
www.belleislebooks.com

To my dear Sloan—
may you always recognize
your inner power.

My mind sometimes races;
it goes and it goes.
It runs this way and that way.
Why? No one knows.

I wonder *What if?*
How come? and *Why did I . . . ?*
I get dizzy watching
my worries fly by.

It might happen in bed,
when Mom turns out the light.
My thinking gets jumbled
and my fears take flight.

Or I'm playing with friends
when out of nowhere—*kaboom!*
My doubts and concerns
are circling the room.

So what do I do
when my mind just won't quit?
The answer is simple:
I breathe and I sit.

I settle right down,
place my hands on my knees;
I sit up real straight,
close my eyes, and I breathe.

Inhale: *one, two, three.*

I'm relaxed and I'm still.

Exhale: *three, two, one.*

No more worries; I'm chill.

As I inhale,
my breath fills up my chest.
I slow down my thinking
and let my mind rest.

When I exhale,
I notice my body feels light.
A power within me
begins to shine bright.

As my breathing slows down,
I feel more in control,
and my burdens and fears
lose their grip on my soul.

I focus and follow
my breath as it flows;
I feel more at peace
from my head to my toes.

My mind feels less scattered.
I'm focused and clear.
By guiding my thoughts,
all my doubts disappear.

The more that I practice,
the easier it gets.
I don't need to carry
these woes and these frets.

By breathing,
I set them aside and feel peace.
By observing,
I find my calm and release.

Days will pass quickly.
There's so much to do.
But my mind can move slower,
if I want it to.

When my thoughts start to spiral
and fill me with dread,
I use my secret power
to clear out my head.

This power within me,
it lives in you too.
You can use it whenever
your troubles find you.

If your mind won't stop racing
and your worries won't leave,
if you're feeling quite anxious,
find your power and breathe.

You don't have to listen
to your doubts any longer.
Their voices are strong,
but you are much stronger.

Breathing Exercises

Three-Count Breath

- Inhale through your nose while slowly counting to three.
  One...
  Two...
  Three...

- Imagine that you are filling a balloon in your chest.

- Exhale through your nose and count from three.
  Three...
  Two...
  One...

- Imagine that you are releasing all the air from that balloon.

- Repeat until you feel relaxed.

Bunny Breath

- Imagine that you are a bunny
  smelling a lovely flower.

- To sniff it, inhale with three quick breaths
  through your bunny nose.
  One.
  Two.
  Three.

- The smell is so sweet and relaxing.
  Now release your breath,
  exhaling through your mouth with a sigh.

- Repeat until you feel calm.

Belly Breath

- Lie down and place a toy
  or stuffed animal on your belly.

- Inhale slowly through your nose
  and watch the object rise.

- Exhale slowly through your nose
  and watch the object fall.

- Continue to focus on the rise and fall
  of your belly until you feel peaceful.

About the Author

MEAGHAN AXEL was a secondary English teacher for many years before her passion for learners and children's literature led her to where she truly belongs—the elementary school library. After dabbling with yoga and meditation for some time, Meaghan became a certified yoga instructor in 2014. She enjoys sharing her love for reading, yoga, and meditation with others. Mrs. Axel lives on the beautiful Eastern Shore of Maryland with her husband and daughter.

About the Illustrator

MICHELLE SIMPSON is a professional illustrator based out of the Niagara Region of Canada. Michelle graduated with a BAA in illustration from Sheridan College, and now works as a freelance illustrator.

Michelle has worked on concept artwork and final backgrounds for season two of the children's TV show *Ollie: The Boy Who Became What He Ate*. She also worked on season one of *Tee and Mo*. Although she takes on many different projects, Michelle's passion is children's book illustration.

CPSIA information can be obtained
at www.ICGtesting.com
Printed in the USA
BVHW021658150919
558452BV00002B/10/P